SPUNK

SPUNK

THREE TALES BY

Zora Neale Hurston

ADAPTED BY

George C. Wolfe

MUSIC BY CHIC STREET MAN

THEATRE COMMUNICATIONS GROUP

1991

Spunk is published by Theatre Communications Group, Inc., 355 Lexington Ave., New York, NY 10017.

TCG gratefully acknowledges public funds from the National Endowment for the Arts and the New York State Council on the Arts in addition to the generous support of the following foundations and corporations: Alcoa Foundation; Ameritech Foundation; ARCO Foundation; AT&T Foundation; Citibank; Common Wealth Fund; ConAgra Charitable Foundation; Consolidated Edison Company of New York; Nathan Cummings Foundation; Eleanor Naylor Dana Charitable Trust; Dayton Hudson Foundation; Exxon Corporation; Ford Foundation; James Irvine Foundation; Jerome Foundation; Andrew W. Mellon Foundation; Metropolitan Life Foundation; National Broadcasting Company; Pew Charitable Trusts; Philip Morris Companies; Reed Foundation; Scherman Foundation; Shell Oil Company Foundation; Shubert Foundation.

Cover: K. Todd Freeman and Danitra Vance in "Story in Harlem Slang." All photographs from the New York Shakespeare Festival production of *Spunk* copyright © 1991 by Martha Swope.

Chic Street Man.
[Spunk. Libretto]
Spunk: three tales / by Zora Neale Hurston; adapted by George C. Wolfe; music by Chic Street Man.
Libretto.
Adaptation of Sweat, Story in Harlem slang, and The gilded six-bits.
Includes the music.
ISBN 1-55936-023-2 (cloth)—ISBN 1-55936-024-0 (pbk.)
1. Musicals—Librettos.   I. Hurston, Zora Neale.   II. Wolfe, George C.   III. Title.
ML50.C537S7   1991   <Case>
782.1′4′0268—dc20   90-29040
                                                          CIP
                                                          MN

Design and composition by The Sarabande Press

First Edition, June 1991

PRODUCTION HISTORY

Spunk was originally developed under the auspices of the Center Theatre Group of Los Angeles at the Mark Taper Forum, Gordon Davidson, Artistic Director. The play was funded in part by a grant from the Rockefeller Foundation.

Spunk had its world premiere at the Crossroads Theatre Company on November 2, 1989. Rick Khan was the Producing Artistic Director. George C. Wolfe directed the following cast:

GUITAR MAN	*Chic Street Man*
BLUES SPEAK WOMAN	*Betty K. Bynum*
THE FOLKS	*Danitra Vance, Reggie Montgomery, Kevin Jackson, Tico Wells*

Loy Arcenas designed the set; Toni-Leslie James, the costumes; Don Holder, the lighting; Hope Clarke, the choreography. David Horton Black was the Production Stage Manager. Sydné Mahone was the Dramaturg.

Spunk opened at Joseph Papp's New York Shakespeare Festival April 18, 1990 with George C. Wolfe directing the following cast:

GUITAR MAN	*Chic Street Man*
BLUES SPEAK WOMAN	*Ann Duquesnay*
THE FOLKS	*Danitra Vance, Reggie Montgomery, Kevin Jackson, K. Todd Freeman*

Loy Arcenas designed the set; Toni-Leslie James, the costumes; Don Holder, the lighting; Barbara Pollitt, the masks and puppets; Hope Clarke, the choreography. Jacqui Casto was the Production Stage Manager.

THE CHARACTERS

Blues Speak Woman
Guitar Man
The Folk, *an acting ensemble of three men and a woman*

TIME

"Round about long 'go"

PLACE

"O, way down nearby"

ACTING STYLE

It is suggested that the rhythms of the dialect be played, instead of the dialect itself. A subtle but important distinction. The former will give you Zora. The latter, Amos and Andy.

The emotional stakes of the characters in the three tales should not be sacrificed for "style." Nor should style be sacrificed because it gets in the way of the emotions. The preferred blend is one in which stylized gesture and speech are fueled by the emotional stakes.

SETTING

The setting is a playing arena, as stark as a Japanese woodcut and as elegant as the blues. The set piece for the three tales should be kept to a minimum so that gesture, lighting, music and the audience's imagination make the picture complete.

Note that throughout the third tale ("The Gilded Six-Bits"), the Players present props which are evocative of the story's shifting locales and time periods. The props should look playful, very used, yet magically simple.

ACT 1

Ann Duquesnay, Reggie Montgomery and Danitra Vance (top) and Danitra Vance and Reggie Montgomery (bottom) in "Sweat" from the New York Shakespeare Festival production.

Prologue

Lights reveal Guitar Man, playing his guitar and whistling, signaling the tales are about to begin. The Folk casually enter, greeting one another. On a musical cue, The Folk freeze and Blues Speak Woman struts on, singing with an earthy elegance.

SONG: GIT TO THE GIT

BLUES SPEAK WOMAN:
OOOOH . . .
HOW DO YOU GIT TO THE GIT?

GUITAR MAN:
HOW DO YOU GIT TO THE GIT?

BLUES SPEAK WOMAN:
I SAY,
HOW DO I GIT TO THE GIT?

GUITAR MAN:
YOU TELL 'EM
HOW TO GIT TO THE GIT?

BLUES SPEAK WOMAN:
WITH SOME BLUES!

GUITAR MAN:
SOME BLUES!

3

BLUES SPEAK WOMAN:
N' SOME GRIT!

GUITAR MAN:
SOME GRIT!

BLUES SPEAK WOMAN:
SOME PAIN!

GUITAR MAN:
PAIN!

BLUES SPEAK WOMAN:
SOME SPIT!

GUITAR MAN:
SPIT!

BLUES SPEAK WOMAN:
N' SOME . . .

BLUES SPEAK WOMAN/GUITAR MAN:
. . . SPUNK!

BLUES SPEAK WOMAN: How yaw doin'? *(With an attitude)* I said how yaw doin'? *(Once the audience responds correctly)* Well all right now! The name is Blues Speak Woman. N' this is Guitar Man. N' these are The Folk!

The Folk ceremoniously bow.

BLUES SPEAK WOMAN: Risk takers!

Presenting themselves.

WOMAN: Heart breakers!

MAN ONE: Masters of emotion!

MAN TWO: Masters of motion!

MAN THREE: N' makers of style.

BLUES SPEAK WOMAN: The three tales we are about to perform, celebrate the laughin' kind of lovin' kind of

hurtin' kind of pain that comes from bein' human. Tales
of survival . . .

TOLD IN THE KEY OF THE BLUES.

Aww, take it away Mr. Guitar Man!

*As Blues Speak Woman/Guitar Man sing, The Folk don
masks, and utilizing dance/gesture, perform the following
scenarios: a man and a woman caught up in the playfulness
of love.*

GUITAR MAN:
> HEY-HEY HEY-HEY
> BABY HEY

BLUES SPEAK WOMAN:
> AWW GIMME SOME OF THAT SPUNK

GUITAR MAN:
> HEY-HEY, HEY-HEY
> BABY HEY

BLUES SPEAK WOMAN:
> AWW GIMME SOME OF THAT SPUNK
> YA GOTS TO GIMME
> GIMME SOME OF THAT SPUNK

*The next scenario: a woman brushing off two men as they try to
put the moves on her.*

BLUES SPEAK WOMAN:
> NO! NO! NO! NO!
> WHAT I GOT YOU AIN'T GONNA GIT

GUITAR MAN:
> Come on now baby,
> Please don't be that way.

BLUES SPEAK WOMAN:

I SAY NO! NO! NO! NO!

WHAT I GOT YOU AIN'T GONNA GIT

GUITAR MAN:

Baby please, I jes' wanna play.

BLUES SPEAK WOMAN:

YO' HAIR MAY BE WAVY,

YO' HEART IS JUST GRAVY

WHAT I GOT YOU AIN'T GONNA GIT!

GUITAR MAN:

NOW THESE FOLK RIDE IN A CADILLAC

N' THOSE FOLK RIDE THE SAME

BUT US FOLK RIDE IN A RUSTY FORD

BUT WE GITS THERE JES' THE SAME

As Blues Speak Woman continues to sing, The Folk set the stage for the first tale.

BLUES SPEAK WOMAN:

AWWW LAUGHIN' . . .

CRYIN'

LOVIN'

FEELIN' ALL KINDSA PAIN

WILL GIT YOU TO THE GIT!

And then the last scenario: a man beating a woman down, until she has no choice but to submit.

BLUES SPEAK WOMAN *(Vocalizing the woman's emotions/pain)*:

AWWWW . . .

AWWWW . . .

AWWWW . . .

(In isolated light.)

GEORGE C. WOLFE

I GIT TO THE GIT
WITH SOME PAIN N' SOME SPIT
N' SOME SPUNK . . . .

The lights crossfade.

TALE NUMBER ONE

"Sweat"

Lights reveal Delia posed over a washtub and surrounded by mounds of white clothes. Music underscore.

BLUES SPEAK WOMAN: It was eleven o'clock of a spring night in Florida. It was Sunday. Any other night Delia Jones would have been in bed . . .

DELIA *(Presenting herself)*: But she was a washwoman.

BLUES SPEAK WOMAN:

AND MONDAY MORNING MEANT A GREAT
  DEAL TO HER.

So she collected the soiled clothes on Saturday, when she returned the clean things.

SUNDAY NIGHT AFTER CHURCH,

she would put the white things to soak.

SHE SQUATTED . . .
SHE SQUATTED . . .

on the kitchen floor beside the great pile of clothes, sorting them into small heaps, and humming . . . humming a song in a joyful key . . .

DELIA: But wondering through it all where her husband, Sykes, had gone with her horse and buckboard.

Lights reveal Sykes, posed at the periphery of the playing arena, a bullwhip in his hand. As he creeps toward Delia . . .

BLUES SPEAK WOMAN: Just then . . .

GUITAR MAN *(Taking up the chant)*:
SYKES . . .
SYKES . . . *(Etc.)*

BLUES SPEAK WOMAN: Something long, round, limp and black fell upon her shoulders and slithered to the floor besides her.

DELIA: A great terror took hold of her!

BLUES SPEAK WOMAN: And then she saw, it was the big bullwhip her husband liked to carry when he drove.

DELIA: Sykes!

Music underscore ends. As the scene between Delia and Sykes is played, Blues Speak Woman and Guitar Man look on.

DELIA: Why you throw dat whip on me like dat? You know it would skeer me—looks just like a snake, an' you know how skeered Ah is of snakes.

SYKES *(Laughing)*: Course Ah knowd it! That's how come Ah done it.

DELIA: You ain't got no business doing it.

SYKES: If you such a big fool dat you got to have a fit over a earth worm or a string, Ah don't keer how bad Ah skeer you.

DELIA *(Simultaneously)*: Gawd knows it's a sin. Some day Ah'm gointuh drop dead from some of yo' foolishness. And another thing!

9

SYKES *(Mocking)*: "'Nother thing."

DELIA: Where you been wid mah rig? Ah feed dat pony. He ain't fuh you to be drivin' wid no bullwhip.

SYKES: You sho' is one aggravatin' nigger woman!

DELIA *(To the audience)*: She resumed her work and did not answer him. *(Humming, she resumes sorting the clothes)*

SYKES: Ah tole you time and again to keep them white folks' clothes outa dis house.

DELIA: Ah ain't for no fuss t'night, Sykes. Ah just come from taking sacrament at the church house.

SYKES: Yeah, you just come from de church house on Sunday night. But heah you is gone to work on them white folks' clothes. You ain't nothing but a hypocrite. One of them amen-corner Christians. Sing, whoop and shout . . . *(Dancing on the clothes)* Oh Jesus! Have mercy! Help me Jesus! Help me!

DELIA: Sykes, quit grindin' dirt into these clothes! How can Ah git through by Sat'day if Ah don't start on Sunday?

SYKES: Ah don't keer if you never git through. Anyhow Ah done promised Gawd and a couple of other men, Ah ain't gointer have it in my house.

Delia is about to speak.

SYKES: Don't gimme no lip either . . .

DELIA: Looka heah Sykes, you done gone too fur.

SYKES *(Overlapping)*: . . . else Ah'll throw 'em out and put mah fist up side yo' head to boot.

Delia finds herself caught in Sykes's grip.

DELIA: Ah been married to you fur fifteen years, and Ah been takin' in washin' fur fifteen years. Sweat, sweat,

sweat! Work and sweat, cry and sweat, and pray and
sweat.

SYKES: What's that got to do with me.

DELIA: What's it got to do with you, Sykes? *(She breaks free of
him)* Mah tub of suds is filled yo' belly with vittles more
times than yo' hands is filled it. Mah sweat is done paid
for this house and Ah reckon Ah kin keep on sweatin' in
it. *(To the audience)* She seized the iron skillet from the
stove and struck a defensive pose.

And that ole snaggle-toothed yella woman you runnin'
with ain't comin' heah to pile up on mah sweat and
blood. You ain't paid for nothin' on this place, and Ah'm
gointer stay right heah till Ah'm toted out foot foremost.

*Musical underscore. Delia maintains her ground, skillet in
hand.*

SYKES: Well, you better quit gittin' me riled up, else they'll
be totin' you out sooner than you expect. Ah'm so tired
of you Ah don't know whut to do. *(To the audience)*
Gawd! How Ah hates skinny wimmen.

He exits.

BLUES SPEAK WOMAN: A little awed by this new Delia, he
sidled out of the door and slammed the back gate after him.
He did not say where he had gone, but she knew too well.
She knew very well that he would not return until nearly
daybreak. Her work over, she went on to bed . . .

DELIA: But not to sleep at once. *(She envelops herself in a sheet,
which becomes her bed)*

BLUES SPEAK WOMAN: She lay awake, gazing upon the

debris that cluttered their matrimonial trail. Not an
image left standing along the way.

DELIA: Anything like flowers had long ago been drowned in
the salty stream that had been pressed from her heart.

BLUE SPEAK WOMAN:
PRESSED FROM HER HEART.

DELIA: Her tears . . .

BLUES SPEAK WOMAN (*Echoing*):
TEARS.

DELIA: Her sweat . . .

BLUES SPEAK WOMAN:
SWEAT.

DELIA: Her blood . . .

BLUES SPEAK WOMAN:
HER BLOOD.

DELIA: She had brought love to the union . . .

BLUES SPEAK WOMAN: And he had brought a longing after
the flesh.

DELIA: Two months after the wedding, he had given her the
first brutal beating.

BLUES SPEAK WOMAN:
SHE WAS YOUNG AND SOFT THEN
SO YOUNG . . .
SO SOFT . . .

DELIA (*Overlapping*): But now she thought of her knotty,
muscled limbs, her harsh knuckly hands, and drew
herself up into an unhappy little ball . . .

BLUE SPEAK WOMAN:
IN THE MIDDLE OF THE BIG FEATHER BED

TOO LATE NOW FOR HOPE,

TOO LATE NOW FOR LOVE,
TOO LATE NOW TO HOPE FOR LOVE,
TOO LATE NOW FOR EVERYTHING

DELIA: Except her little home. She had built it for her old days, and planted one by one the trees and flowers there.

BLUES SPEAK WOMAN:

IT WAS LOVELY TO HER

DELIA: Lovely.

BLUES SPEAK WOMAN:

LOVELY . . .

Somehow before sleep came, she found herself saying aloud—

DELIA: Oh well, whatever goes over the Devil's back, is got to come under his belly. Sometime or ruther, Sykes, like everybody else, is gonna reap his sowing.

BLUES SPEAK WOMAN: Amen! She went to sleep and slept.

Music underscore ends.

BLUES SPEAK WOMAN: Until he announced his presence in bed.

Sykes enters.

DELIA: By kicking her feet and rudely snatching the covers away.

As he grabs the sheet, blackout. Lights isolate Guitar Man. Music underscore.

GUITAR MAN: People git ready for Joe Clarke's Porch. Cane chewin'! People watchin'! Nuthin' but good times, on Joe Clarke's Porch.

Lights reveal the men on the porch, Man One and Two. Sitting between them, a life-size puppet, Joe Clarke. The men on the porch scan the horizon, their movements staccato and stylized. Upon seeing an imaginary woman walk past . . .

MEN ON PORCH: Aww sookie! Sookie! Sookie! *(Ad lib)* Come here gal! Git on back here! Woman wait!

The "woman" continues on her way as the morning heat settles in.

MAN TWO: It was a hot, hot day . . . near the end of July.

MAN ONE: The village men on Joe Clarke's porch even chewed cane . . . listlessly.

MAN TWO: What do ya say we . . . naw!

MAN ONE: How's about we . . . naw!

MAN TWO: Even conversation . . .

MAN ONE: Had collapsed under the heat.

Music underscore ends.

MAN TWO: "Heah come Delia Jones," Jim Merchant said, as the shaggy pony came 'round the bend of the road toward them.

MAN ONE: The rusty buckboard heaped with baskets of crisp, clean laundry.

MAN ONE/TWO: Yep.

MAN ONE: Hot or col', rain or shine, jes'ez reg'lar ez de weeks roll roun', Delia carries 'em an' fetches 'em on Sat'day.

MAN TWO: She better if she wanter eat. Sykes Jones ain't wuth de shot an' powder it would tek tuh kill 'em. Not to huh he ain't.

MAN ONE: He sho' ain't. It's too bad, too, cause she wuz a right pretty li'l trick when he got huh. Ah'd uh mah'ied huh mahself if he hadnter beat me to it.

Joe Clarke scoffs at Man One's claim.

MAN ONE: That's the truth Joe.

BLUES SPEAK WOMAN: Delia nodded briefly at the men as she drove past.

The men tip their hats and bow.

MAN ONE/TWO: How ya do Delia.

MAN TWO: Too much knockin' will ruin any 'oman. He done beat huh 'nough tuh kill three women, let 'lone change they looks. How Sykes kin stommuck dat big, fat, greasy Mogul he's layin' roun' wid, gets me. What's hur name? Bertha?

MAN ONE: She's fat, thass how come. He's allus been crazy 'bout fat women. He'd a' been tied up wid one long time ago if he could a' found one tuh have him. Did Ah tell yuh 'bout him sidlin' roun' mah wife—bringin' her a basket uh pecans outa his yard fuh a present?

MAN TWO: There oughter be a law about him. He ain't fit tuh carry guts tuh a bear.

GUITAR MAN: Joe Clarke spoke for the first time.

Music underscore.

BLUES SPEAK WOMAN *(The voice of Joe Clarke)*: Tain't no law on earth dat kin make a man be decent if it ain't in 'im.

MAN ONE/TWO: *(Ad lib)*: Speak the truth Joe. Tell it! Tell it!

BLUES SPEAK WOMAN *(As Joe Clarke)*: Now-now-now, there's plenty men dat takes a wife lak dey a joint uh sugar-cane. It's round, juicy an' sweet when dey gits it. But dey squeeze an' grind, squeeze an' grind an' wring tell dey wrings every drop uh pleasure dat's in 'em out. When dey's satisfied dat dey is wrung dry . . .

MAN ONE: What dey do Joe?

BLUES SPEAK WOMAN *(As Joe Clarke)*: Dey treats 'em jes' lak dey do a cane-chew. Throws 'em away! Now-now-now-now, dey knows whut dey's doin' while dey's at it, an' hates theirselves fur it. But they keeps on hangin' after huh tell she's empty. Den dey hates huh fuh bein' a cane-chew an' in de way.

MAN ONE: We oughter take Syke an' dat stray 'oman uh his'n down in Lake Howell swamp an' lay on de rawhide till they cain't say Lawd a' mussy.

MAN TWO: We oughter kill 'em!

MAN ONE: A grunt of approval went around the porch.

MEN: Umhmm, umhmm, umhmm.

MAN TWO: But the heat was melting their civic virtue.

MAN ONE: Elijah Mosley began to bait Joe Clarke.

Come on Joe, git a melon outa dere an' slice it up for yo' customers. We'se all sufferin' wid de heat. De bear's done got me!

BLUES SPEAK WOMAN *(As Joe Clarke)*: Yaw gimme twenty cents and slice away.

MAN ONE · TWO *(Ad lib)*: Twenty cents! I give you a nickel. Git it on out here Joe . . . *(Etc.)*

BLUES SPEAK WOMAN: The money was all quickly subscribed and the huge melon brought forth. At that moment . . .

SYKES: Sykes and Bertha arrived . . .

Blues Speak Woman dons a hand-held mask and becomes Bertha.

MAN ONE: A determined silence fell on the porch.

MAN TWO: And the melon was put away.

BLUES SPEAK WOMAN *(Lifting the Bertha mask)*: Just then . . .

Delia enters.

DELIA: Delia drove past on her way home, as Sykes . . .

SYKES: Was ordering magnificently for Bertha.

He kisses Bertha's hand. She squeals.

SYKES: It pleased him for Delia to see this.
 Git whutsoever yo' heart desires, Honey. Give huh two bottles uh strawberry soda-water . . .

Bertha squeals.

SYKES: Uh quart parched ground-peas . . .

Bertha squeals.

SYKES: An' a block uh chewin' gum.

DELIA: With all this they left the store.

SYKES: Sykes reminding Bertha that this was his town . . .

Man One makes a move to go after Sykes. Joe Clarke restrains him.

SYKES: And she could have it if she wanted it.

Music underscore ends. As Sykes and Bertha exit . . .

MAN ONE: Where did Syke Jones git da stray 'oman from nohow?

MAN TWO: Ovah Apopka. Guess dey musta been cleanin' out de town when she lef'. She don't look lak a thing but a hunk uh liver wid hair on it.

MAN ONE *(Laughing)*: Well, she sho' kin squall. When she gits ready tuh laff, she jes' opens huh mouf an' latches it back tuh de las' notch. No ole granpa alligator down in Lake Bell ain't got nothin' on huh.

Music underscore. In isolated pools of light, the men on the porch, Delia and Sykes.

GUITAR MAN:
SWEAT . . .
SWEAT . . .

BLUES SPEAK WOMAN: Bertha had been in town three months now.

MAN TWO: Sykes was still paying her room-rent at Della Lewis'.

MAN ONE: Naw!

MAN TWO: The only house in town that would have taken her in.

MAN ONE: Delia avoided the villagers and meeting places in her efforts to be blind and deaf.

MAN TWO: But Bertha nullified this to a degree, by coming to Delia's house to call Sykes out to her at the gate!

Delia is seen listening as Sykes talks to the audience as if they were Bertha.

SYKES: Sho' you kin have dat li'l ole house soon's Ah git dat 'oman outa dere. Everything b'longs tuh me an' you sho' kin have it. You kin git anything you wants. Dis is mah town an' you sho' kin have it.

BLUES SPEAK WOMAN:

> THE SUN HAD BURNED JULY TO AUGUST
> THE HEAT STREAMED DOWN
> LIKE A MILLION HOT ARROWS
> SMITING ALL THINGS LIVING UPON THE
> EARTH

> Grass withered! Leaves browned! Snakes went blind in shedding! And men and dogs went mad. *(Eyeing Sykes)* Dog days.

GUITAR MAN:

> SYKES . . .
> SYKES . . .

Sykes surreptitiously places a wire-covered soap box, and covers it with the mound of clothes.

BLUES SPEAK WOMAN: Delia came home one day and found Sykes there before her. She noticed a soap box beside the steps, but paid no particular attention to it.

SYKES: Look in de box dere Delia, Ah done brung yuh somethin'.

BLUES SPEAK WOMAN: When she saw what it held . . .

Delia crosses to the box and lifts the lid. Lights reveal the men on the porch. With rattlers in hand, they produce the sound of a snake's rattle.

DELIA: Syke! Syke, mah Gawd! You take dat rattlesnake 'way from heah! You gottuh. Oh Jesus, have mussy!

SYKES: Ah ain't got tuh do nuthin' uh de kin'—fact is Ah ain't got tuh do nuthin' but die.

Sound of the snake's rattle.

DELIA: Naw, now Syke, don't keep dat thing 'round tryin' tuh skeer me tuh death. You knows Ah'm even feared uh earth worms.

SYKES: Tain't no use uh you puttin' on airs makin' out lak you skeered uh dat snake. He wouldn't risk breakin' out his fangs 'gin yo' skinny laigs nohow. He's gointer stay right heah tell he die. Now he wouldn't bite me cause Ah knows how to handle 'im.

DELIA: Kill 'im Syke, please.

SYKES (*Staring transfixed into the box*): Naw, Ah ain't gonna kill it. Ah think uh damn sight mo' uh him dan you! Dat's a nice snake.

Sykes turns to find Delia standing over him ready to strike him. He lifts the lid to the snake box—she backs away.

SYKES: An anybody doan lak it, kin jes' hit de grit.

BLUES SPEAK WOMAN: The snake stayed on.

MAN ONE: The snake stayed on.

MAN TWO: The snake stayed on.

As Delia continues to speak, Sykes stalks the playing arena, waiting for her to "break."

DELIA: His box remained by the kitchen door. It rattled at every movement in the kitchen or the yard.

BLUES SPEAK WOMAN: One day Delia came down the kitchen steps. She saw his chalky-white fangs curved like scimitars hung in the wire meshes. This time she did not run away with averted eyes as usual. She stood for a long time in the doorway . . .

DELIA: In a red fury that grew bloodier for every second that she regarded the creature that was her torment.

BLUES SPEAK WOMAN: That night she broached the subject as soon as Sykes sat down to the table.

DELIA: Sykes!

Music underscore ends. As the scene between Delia and Sykes is played, Blues Speak Woman and Guitar Man look on.

DELIA: Ah wants you tuh take dat snake 'way fum heah. You done starved me an' Ah put up widcher. You done beat me an Ah took dat. But you done kilt all mah insides bringin' dat varmint heah.

SYKES *(To the audience)*: Sykes poured out a saucer full of coffee and drank it deliberately before he answered.

A whole lot Ah keer 'bout how you feels inside uh out. Dat snake ain't goin' no damn wheah till Ah gets ready fuh 'im tuh go. So fur as beatin' is concerned, yuh ain't took near all dat you gointer take if yuh stay 'round me.

DELIA: Delia pushed back her plate and got up from the table.

Ah hates you, Sykes. Ah hates you tuh de same degree dat Ah useter love yuh. Ah done took an' took till mah belly is full up tuh mah neck. Dat's de reason Ah got mah letter fum de church an' moved mah membership tuh Woodbridge—so Ah don't haftuh take no sacrament wid yuh. Ah don't wantuh see yuh 'round me atall. Lay 'round wid dat 'oman all yuh wants tuh, but gwan 'way fum me an' mah house. Ah hates yuh lak uh suck-egg dog!

SYKES: Well, Ah'm glad you does hate me. Ah'm sho' tiahed uh you hangin' ontuh me. Ah don't want yuh. Look at yuh stringy ole neck! Yo' rawbony laigs an' arms is enough tuh cut uh man tuh death. You look jes' lak de devvul's doll-baby tuh me. You cain't hate me no worse dan Ah hates you. Ah been hatin' you fuh years.

DELIA: Yo' ole black hide don't look lak nothin' tuh me, but uh passle uh wrinkled up rubber, wid yo' big ole yeahs flappin' on each side lak uh paih uh buzzard wings. Don't think Ah'm gointuh be run 'way fum mah house neither. Ah'm goin' tuh de white folks 'bout you, mah young man, de very nex' time you lay yo' han's on me.

She pushes him. He grabs her. She breaks free.

DELIA: Mah cup is done run ovah!
　　　Sykes departed from the house!

Sykes abruptly turns to exit, but his rage takes hold and he comes charging back, ready to hit her.

DELIA: Threatening her!

Just as he is about to hit Delia, he stops, regains control of his emotions and gently kisses her.

SYKES (*Smiling*): But he made not the slightest move to carry out any of them.

He exits.

BLUES SPEAK WOMAN: That night he did not return at all. And the next day being Sunday . . .

Music underscore. Lights reveal the men on the porch, swaying to the gospel beat.

DELIA: Delia was glad she did not have to quarrel before she hitched up her pony and drove the four miles to Woodbridge.

BLUES SPEAK WOMAN: She stayed to the night service which was very warm and full of spirit. As she drove homeward she sang.

DELIA:

JURDEN WATER

BLUES SPEAK WOMAN/MEN ON PORCH:

JURDEN WATER

DELIA:

BLACK N' COLD

WOMAN/MEN:

BLACK N' COLD

DELIA:

CHILLS THE BODY

WOMAN/MEN:

CHILLS THE BODY

DELIA:

BUT NOT THE SOUL

WOMAN/MEN:

NOT THE SOUL

DELIA:

SAID I WANNA CROSS JURDEN

WOMAN/MEN:

CROSS OVER JURDEN

DELIA:

IN A CALM . . .

WOMAN/MEN:

CALM TIME, CALM TIME, CALM TIME

DELIA:

TIME . . .

Men on porch repeat the "calm time" refrain as the action continues.

BLUES SPEAK WOMAN: She came from the barn to the kitchen door and stopped and addressed the snake's box.

DELIA: Whut's de mattah, ol' Satan, you ain't kickin' up yo' racket. *(She kicks the snake box)*

BLUES SPEAK WOMAN: Complete silence.

DELIA: Perhaps her threat to go to the white folks had frightened Sykes. Perhaps he was sorry.

BLUES SPEAK WOMAN: She decided she need not bring the hamper out of the bedroom; she would go in there and do the sorting. So she picked up the pot-bellied lamp and went in.

DELIA: The room was small and the hamper stood hard by the foot of the white iron bed.

BLUES SPEAK WOMAN *(A gospel riff)*:

SAID I WANTAH CROSS JURDEN

Men on porch/Guitar Man add in.

WOMAN/MEN/GUITAR:

IN CALM . . .

Delia screams.

DELIA: There lay the snake in the basket!

BLUES SPEAK WOMAN: She saw him pouring his awful beauty from the basket upon the bed. The wind from the open door blew out the light. She sped to the darkness of the yard, slamming the door after her before she thought to set down the lamp. She did not feel safe even on the ground. So she climbed up into the hay barn.

DELIA (*Sitting atop a ladder*): Finally she grew quiet. And with this stalked through her a cold, bloody rage. She went to sleep . . . a twitch sleep. And woke to a faint gray sky.

BLUES SPEAK WOMAN: There was a loud, hollow sound below. She peered out . . .

DELIA/BLUES SPEAK WOMAN: Sykes!

Sykes abruptly appears.

SYKES: . . . was at the wood-pile, demolishing a wire-covered box. He hurried to the kitchen door, but hung outside there some minutes before he entered and stood some minutes more inside before he closed it after him.

No mo' skinny women! No mo' white folks' clothes. This is my house! *My* house!

DELIA: Delia descended without fear now . . .

BLUES SPEAK WOMAN: And crouched beneath the low bedroom window. The drawn shade shut out the dawn, shut in the night, but the thin walls . . .

MAN ONE: Held . . .

MAN TWO: Back . . .

DELIA: No . . .

BLUES SPEAK WOMAN: Sound. Inside, Sykes heard nothing until he—

SYKES: Knocked a pot lid off the stove.

DELIA: Trying to reach the match-safe in the dark.

Music underscore. Men on porch create sound of the snake rattle. Sykes stops dead in his tracks.

SYKES (*Leaping onto a chair*): Sykes made a quick leap into the bedroom.

BLUES SPEAK WOMAN: The rattling ceased for a moment as he stood . . .

SYKES: Paralyzed. He waited.

BLUES SPEAK WOMAN (*Sardonically*): It seemed that the snake waited also.

With regained composure, Sykes gets down from the chair and cautiously moves about.

SYKES: Where you at? Humm. Wherever that is, stay there while I . . .

DELIA: Sykes was muttering to himself . . .

BLUES SPEAK WOMAN: When the whirr began again.

Sound of snake's rattle and music underscore.

SYKES: Closer, right underfoot this time. He leaped—onto the bed.

In isolated light, the actor playing Sykes becomes both Sykes and the snake.

DELIA: Outside Delia heard a cry.

Sykes cries out in pain.

MAN ONE: A tremendous stir inside!

MAN TWO: Another series of animal screams!

Sykes cries out.

MAN ONE: A huge brown hand seizing the window stick!

MAN TWO: Great dull blows upon the wooden floor!

MAN ONE: Punctuating the gibberish of sound long after the rattle of the snake . . .

MAN TWO: Had abruptly subsided.

Music underscore ends.

BLUES SPEAK WOMAN: All this Delia could see and hear from her place beneath the window. And it made her ill. She crept over to the four-o'clocks and stretched herself on the cool earth to recover.

Music underscore. As Blues Speak Woman talks/sings, Sykes crawls toward Delia. Meanwhile, the men on the porch scan the horizon, signaling the beginning of a new day.

BLUES SPEAK WOMAN: She lay there. She could hear Sykes . . .

CALLING IN A MOST DESPAIRING TONE

As one who expected no answer.

THE SUN CREPT ON UP . . .

And he called.
Delia could not move. She never moved.
He called

AND THE SUN KEPT ON RISIN'
   "MAH GAWD!"
SHE HEARD HIM MOAN
   "MAH GAWD FROM HEBBEN."

She heard him stumbling about and got up from her flower bed.

THE SUN WAS GROWING WARM.

The music ends.

SYKES: Delia, is dat you Ah heah?

BLUES SPEAK WOMAN: She saw him on his hands and knees. His horribly swollen neck, his one eye open, shining with . . .

SYKES: Hope.

Sykes extends his hand toward Delia. The weight and desperation of his grip pulls her to the ground. She is about to console him, but instead, scurries away.

DELIA: A surge of pity too strong to support bore her away from that eye . . .

BLUES SPEAK WOMAN: That must, could not, fail to see the lamp.

DELIA: Orlando with its doctors . . .

BLUES SPEAK WOMAN: Oh it's too far!

Sykes grabs hold to the hem of her dress. Delia calmly steps beyond his reach.

DELIA: She could scarcely reach the chinaberry tree, where she waited . . . in the growing heat . . .

BLUES SPEAK WOMAN: While inside she knew, the cold river was creeping up . . . creeping up to extinguish that eye which must know by now that she knew.

Music underscore. Delia looks on as Sykes recoils into a fetal position and dies. The sound of the snake's rattle as she looks at the audience.

DELIA: Sweat!

Blackout.

SONG: I'VE BEEN LIVING WITH THE BLUES

In isolated light, Guitar Man.

GUITAR MAN: Not everybody's got a snake in they house,
but we all gits the blues.

ROCKS IS MY PILLOW
COLD GROUND MY BED
BLUE SKIES MY BLANKET
MOONLIGHT MY SPREAD
I'M NOT ASHAMED
AIN'T THAT NEWS
I BEEN LIVIN' WITH THE BLUES

I WORKS ALL SUMMER
I SLEEPS ALL FALL
I SPEND MY CHRISTMAS
IN MY OVERALLS
I'M NOT ASHAMED
HONEY AIN'T THAT NEWS
I BEEN LIVIN' WITH THE BLUES

Music interlude.

OOH, ROCKS HAS BEEN MY PILLOW
COLD GROUND HAS BEEN MY BED
BLUE SKIES HAVE BEEN MY BLANKET
AND THE MOONLIGHT HAS BEEN MY SPREAD

IF YOU'VE EVER BEEN DOWN
YOU KNOW JUST HOW I FEEL
I FEEL LIKE AN ENGINE
GOT NO DRIVIN' WHEEL

I'M NOT ASHAMED
NUTHIN' NEW
I BEEN LIVIN' WITH THE BLUES

MY MOMMA HAD 'EM
MY DADDY HAD 'EM TOO
YES HE DID
YOU SEE, I BEEN LIVIN' WITH THE BLUES

ALL YOU PEOPLE
OUT THERE TOO
YES YOU HAVE
WE ALL BEEN LIVIN' WITH THE BLUES

Three panels, suggestive of 1940s *Harlem, drop onto the stage. Blues Speak Woman struts on, her accessories and attitude are Harlem highbrow, with a touch of the "low." Guitar Man likes what he sees, and so the game begins.*

SONG: HEY BABY

GUITAR MAN:

HEY BABY,
SAY BABY HOW DO YOU DO?

BLUES SPEAK WOMAN: You talkin' to me?

GUITAR MAN:

YEAH BABY,
SAY BABY HOW DO YOU DO?
TELL ME HOW DO YOU DO
SO I CAN DO A LITTLE BIT WITH YOU

BLUES SPEAK WOMAN: Do what with who?

GUITAR MAN: With you sweet mama, with you.

BLUES SPEAK WOMAN (*Walking toward him*):

YEAH I'M LOOKIN',

LOOKIN' EVERYWHERE I GO
YEAH I'M LOOKIN',
LOOKIN' BOTH HIGH N' LOW
AND WHEN I LOOK AT YOU . . .

GUITAR MAN: What you see baby?

BLUES SPEAK WOMAN:

I SEE I GOTS TO LOOK SOME MO'!

She walks away. He calls after her.

GUITAR MAN:

HEY BABY,
WHO DO YOU THINK I AM?

BLUES SPEAK WOMAN::

HEY BABY,
WHO DO YOU THINK I AM?
I'M JUST A FINE FRAIL RAIL

GUITAR MAN:

AND I'M HOT AS JULY JAM

(Moving in for the kill)

HEY BABY,
I'D LIKE TO LAY NOW NEXT TO YOU

BLUES SPEAK WOMAN:

WELL, MAYBE,
I'D LIKE TO . . . NEXT TO YOU TOO

BLUES SPEAK WOMAN/GUITAR MAN:

BUT I'M SO GOOD LOOKIN'

BLUES SPEAK WOMAN:

I SAID I'M GOOD LOOKIN'

GUITAR MAN:

I'M GOOD LOOKIN'!

BLUES SPEAK WOMAN: Don't you bull-skate me baby cause just look at this! Look at this! If you lookin' for a dusty butt, Beluthahatchie is that way 'n' that way. Any way but this way.

CAUSE IT DON'T GIT!
NO IT DON'T GIT
IT DON'T GIT NO BETTER . . . THAN THIS

GUITAR MAN: No baby, don't *you* bull-skate *me*. Cause I'm fine as wine. I say I'm fine as wine. Randy, dandy and handy, smooth like brandy.

I COME ON LIGHTLY
SLIGHTLY . . .
AND OOOOOOH, SO POLITELY
IN OTHER WORDS . . .

BLUES SPEAK WOMAN/GUITAR MAN:
I'M TOO GOOD LOOKIN' FOR YOU!

They turn to go in opposite directions, stop and then look back.

BLUES SPEAK WOMAN/GUITAR MAN: But then again . . .

Fade to black.

"Story in Harlem Slang"

Lights reveal Slang Talk Man: his attire, very debonair; his manner of speaking, very smooth.

SLANG TALK MAN: Wait till I light up my coal-pot and tell you about this Zigaboo called Jelly.

On Slang Talk Man's signal, lights reveal Jelly, a hick trying to pass himself off as slick. He wears a stocking cap and underneath his "street" bravado is a boyish charm.

JELLY: Well all right now!

SLANG TALK MAN: He was sealskin brown and papa-tree-top tall.

JELLY: Skinny in the hips and solid built for speed.

SLANG TALK MAN: He was born with this rough-dried hair, but when he laid on the grease and pressed it down overnight with his stocking-cap . . .

Jelly pulls off the cap to admire his "do."

JELLY: It looked just like righteous moss.

SLANG TALK MAN: Had so many waves, you got seasick
    from lookin'.

JELLY: Solid man solid.

SLANG TALK MAN: His mama named him Marvel, but after
    a month on Lenox Avenue . . .

*On Slang Talk Man's signal, a zoot-suit jacket and hat
magically appear.*

SLANG TALK MAN: He changed all that to—

JELLY *(Getting dressed)*: Jelly.

SLANG TALK MAN: How come? Well he put it in the street
    that when it comes to filling that long-felt need . . .

JELLY: Sugar-curing the ladies' feelings . . .

SLANG TALK MAN: He was in a class by himself. And
    nobody knew his name, so he had to tell 'em.

JELLY: It must be Jelly cause jam don't shake!

SLANG TALK MAN: That was what was on his sign. The
    stuff was there and it was mellow. N' whenever he was
    challenged by a hard-head or a frail eel on the right of
    his title, he would eyeball the idol-breaker with a slice of
    ice and say—

JELLY: Youse just dumb to the fact, baby. If you don't know
    what you talking 'bout, you better ask Granny Grunt. I
    wouldn't mislead you baby. I don't need to. Not with the
    help I got.

SLANG TALK MAN: Then he would give the pimp's sign . . .

*Jelly/Slang Talk Man adopt an exaggerated "street" pose; for
Slang Talk Man it's empty posturing; for Jelly it's the real
deal.*

SLANG TALK MAN: And percolate on down the Avenue.

On Slang Talk Man's signal, the Footnote Voice is heard. As the Voice speaks, Jelly practices a series of poses.

FOOTNOTE VOICE: Please note. In Harlemese, pimp has a different meaning than its ordinary definition. The Harlem pimp is a man whose amatory talents are for sale to any woman who will support him, either with a free meal or on a common-law basis; in this sense, he is actually a male prostitute.

SLANG TALK MAN: So this day he was airing out on the Avenue. It had to be late afternoon, or he would not have been out of bed.

JELLY: Shoot, all you did by rolling out early was to stir your stomach up. *(Confidentially)* That made you hunt for more dishes to dirty. The longer you slept, the less you had to eat.

SLANG TALK MAN: But you can't collar nods all day. So Jelly . . .

Music underscore.

SLANG TALK MAN: Got into his zoot suit with the reet pleats and got out to skivver around and do himself some good.

The transformation from "Jelly the Hick" into "Jelly the Slick" is now complete. He struts and poses like a tiger on the prowl; his moves suggestive, arrogant, mocking.

Lights reveal Blues Speak Woman and Guitar Man, sitting outside the playing arena, scatting vocalise which accents Jelly's moves.

JELLY: No matter how long you stay in bed, and how quiet you keep, sooner or later that big guts is going to reach over and grab that little one and start to gnaw. That's confidential from the Bible. You got to get out on the beat and collar yourself a hot!

SLANG TALK MAN: At 132nd Street, he spied one of his colleagues, Sweet Back! Standing on the opposite sidewalk, in front of a café.

Lights reveal Sweet Back, older than Jelly; the wear and tear of the street is starting to reveal itself in Sweet Back's face. Nonetheless, he moves with complete finesse as he and Jelly stalk each other, each trying to outdo the other as they strut, pose and lean.

SLANG TALK MAN: Jelly figured that if he bull-skated just right, he might confidence Sweet Back out of a thousand on a plate. Maybe a shot of scrap-iron or a reefer. Therefore, they both took a quick backward look at the soles of their shoes to see how their leather was holding out. They then stanched out into the street and made the crossing.

Music underscore ends.

JELLY: Hey there, Sweet Back. Gimme some skin!

SWEET BACK: Lay the skin on me pal. Ain't seen you since the last time, Jelly. What's cookin'?

JELLY: Oh, just like the bear, I ain't no where. Like the bear's brother, I ain't no further. Like the bear's daughter, ain't got a quarter.

SLANG TALK MAN: Right away he wished he had not been so honest. Sweet Back gave him a—

SWEET BACK: Top-superior, cut-eye look.

SLANG TALK MAN: Looked at Jelly just like—

SWEET BACK: A showman looks at an ape.

SLANG TALK MAN: Just as far above Jelly as fried chicken is over branch water.

SWEET BACK: Cold in the hand huh? A red hot pimp like you say you is ain't got no business in the barrel. Last night when I left you, you was beating up your gums and broadcasting about how hot you was. Just as hot as July jam, you told me. What you doin' cold in hand?

JELLY: Aw man, can't you take a joke? I was just beating up my gums when I said I was broke. How can I be broke when I got the best woman in Harlem? If I ask her for a dime, she'll give me a ten dollar bill. Ask her for a drink of likker, and she'll buy me a whiskey still. If I'm lyin' I'm flyin'!

SWEET BACK: Man, don't hang out that dirty washing in my back yard. Didn't I see you last night with that beat chick, scoffing a hot dog? That chick you had was beat to the heels. Boy, you ain't no good for what you live. And you ain't got nickel one. *(As if to a passing woman)* Hey baby!

SLANG TALK MAN: Jelly—

JELLY: Threw back the long skirt of his coat.

SLANG TALK MAN: And rammed his hand into his pants pocket. Sweet Back—

SWEET BACK: Made the same gesture . . .

SLANG TALK MAN: Of hauling out non-existent money.

JELLY: Put your money where your mouth is. Back yo' crap with your money. I bet you five dollars.

SWEET BACK: Oh yeah!

JELLY: Yeah.

Jelly/Sweet Back move toward each other, wagging their pants pockets at each other.

SWEET BACK *(Playfully)*: Jelly-Jelly-Jelly. I been raised in the church. I don't bet. But I'll doubt you. Five rocks!

JELLY: I thought so. *(Loud talking)* I knowed he'd back up when I drawed my roll on him.

SWEET BACK: You ain't drawed no roll on me, Jelly. You ain't drawed nothing but your pocket. *(With an edge)* You better stop that boogerbooing. Next time I'm liable to make you do it.

SLANG TALK MAN: There was a splinter of regret in Sweet Back's voice. If Jelly really had had some money, he might have staked him to a hot.

SWEET BACK: Good Southern cornbread with a piano on a platter.

SLANG TALK MAN: Oh well! The right broad would . . . might come along.

JELLY: Who boogerbooing? Jig, I don't have to. Talkin' about me with a beat chick scoffing a hot dog? Man you musta not seen me, 'cause last night I was riding 'round in a Yellow Cab, with a yellow gal, drinking yellow likker and spending yellow money. *(To the audience)* Tell 'em 'bout me. You was there. Tell 'em!

SWEET BACK: Git out of my face Jelly! That broad I seen you with wasn't no pe-ola. She was one of them coal-scuttle blondes with hair just as close to her head as ninety-nine to hundred. She look-ted like she had seventy-five pounds of clear bosom, and she look-ted like six months in front and nine months behind. Buy you a whiskey still! That broad couldn't make the down payment on a pair of sox.

JELLY: Naw-naw-naw-now Sweet Back, long as you been knowing me, you ain't never seen me with nothing but pe-olas. I can get any frail eel I wants to. How come I'm up here in New York? Huh-huh-huh? You don't know, do you? Since youse dumb to the fact, I reckon I'll have to make you hep. I had to leave from down south cause Miss Anne used to worry me so bad to go with her. Who me? Man, I don't deal in no coal.

SWEET BACK: Aww man, you trying to show your grandma how to milk ducks. Best you can do is confidence some kitchen-mechanic out of a dime or two. Me, I knocks the pad with them cackbroads up on Sugar Hill and fills 'em full of melody. Man, I'm quick death 'n' easy judgment. You just a home-boy, Jelly. Don't try to follow me.

JELLY: Me follow you! Man, I come on like the Gang Busters and go off like The March of Time. If that ain't so, God is gone to Jersey City and you know He wouldn't be messing 'round a place like that.

SLANG TALK MAN: Looka there!

Sweet Back/Jelly scurry and look.

SLANG TALK MAN: Oh well, the right broad might come along.

JELLY: Know what my woman done? We hauled off and went to church last Sunday. And when they passed 'round the plate for the penny collection, I throwed in a dollar. The man looked at me real hard for that. That made my woman mad, so she called him back and throwed in a twenty dollar bill. Told him to take that and go! That's what he got for looking at me 'cause I throwed in a dollar.

SWEET BACK: Jelly . . .

The wind may blow
And the door may slam.
That what you shooting
Ain't worth a damn!

JELLY: Sweet Back you fixing to talk out of place.

SWEET BACK: If you tryin' to jump salty Jelly, that's yo' mammy.

JELLY: Don't play in the family Sweet Back. I don't play the dozens. I done told you.

SLANG TALK MAN: Jelly—

JELLY: Slammed his hand in his bosom as if to draw a gun.

SLANG TALK MAN: Sweet Back—

SWEET BACK: Did the same.

JELLY: If you wants to fight, Sweet Back, the favor is in me.

Jelly/Sweet Back begin to circle one another, each waiting on the other to "strike" first.

SWEET BACK: I was deep-thinking then, Jelly. It's a good thing I ain't short-tempered. Tain't nothing to you nohow.

JELLY: Oh yeah. Well, come on.

SWEET BACK: No you come on.

SWEET BACK/JELLY *(Overlapping)*: Come on! Come on! Come on! Come on!

They are now in each other's face, grimacing, snarling, ready to fight, when Sweet Back throws Jelly a look.

SWEET BACK: You ain't hit me yet.

They both begin to laugh, which grows, until they are falling all over each other: the best of friends.

SWEET BACK: Don't get too yaller on me Jelly. You liable to get hurt some day.

JELLY: You over-sports your hand yo' ownself. Too blamed astorperious. I just don't pay you no mind. Lay the skin on me man.

SLANG TALK MAN: They broke their handshake hurriedly, because both of them looked up the Avenue and saw the same thing.

SWEET BACK/JELLY: It was a girl.

Music underscore as lights reveal the girl, busily posing and preening.

SLANG TALK MAN: And they both remembered that it was Wednesday afternoon. All the domestics off for the afternoon with their pay in their pockets.

SWEET BACK/JELLY: Some of them bound to be hungry for love.

SLANG TALK MAN: That meant . . .

SWEET BACK: Dinner!

JELLY: A shot of scrap-iron!

SWEET BACK: Maybe room rent!

JELLY: A reefer or two!

SLANG TALK MAN: They both . . .

SWEET BACK: Went into the pose.

JELLY: And put on the look. *(Loud talking)* Big stars falling.

SLANG TALK MAN: Jelly said out loud when the girl was in hearing distance.

JELLY: It must be just before day!

SWEET BACK: Yeah man. Must be recess in Heaven, pretty angel like that out on the ground.

SLANG TALK MAN: The girl drew abreast of them, reeling and rocking her hips.

Blues Speak Woman scats as the girl struts, her hips working to the beat of the music. Jelly and Sweet Back swoop in and begin their moves.

JELLY: I'd walk clear to Diddy-Wah-Diddy to get a chance to speak to a pretty li'l ground-angel like that.

SWEET BACK: Aw, man you ain't willing to go very far. Me, I'd go slap to Ginny-Gall, where they eat cow-rump, skin and all.

SLANG TALK MAN: The girl smiled, so Jelly set his hat and took the plunge.

JELLY: Ba-by, what's on de rail for de lizard?

SLANG TALK MAN: The girl halted and braced her hips with her hands.

Music underscore stops.

GIRL: A Zigaboo down in Georgy, where I come from, asked a woman that one time and the judge told him ninety days.

Music underscore continues.

SWEET BACK: Georgy! Where 'bouts in Georgy you from? Delaware?

JELLY: Delaware? My people! My people! Man, how you going to put Delaware in Georgy. You ought to know that's in Maryland.

Music underscore stops.

GIRL: Oh, don't try to make out youse no northerner, you! Youse from right down in 'Bam your ownself.

JELLY: Yeah, I'm *from* there and I aims to stay from there.

GIRL: One of them Russians, eh? Rushed up here to get away from a job of work.

Music underscore continues.

SLANG TALK MAN: That kind of talk was not leading towards the dinner table.

JELLY: But baby! That shape you got on you! I bet the Coca-Cola company is paying you good money for the patent!

SLANG TALK MAN: The girl smiled with pleasure at this, so Sweet Back jumped in.

SWEET BACK: I know youse somebody swell to know. Youse real people. There's dickty jigs 'round here tries to smile. You grins like a regular fellow.

SLANG TALK MAN: He gave her his most killing look and let it simmer.

SWEET BACK: S'pose you and me go inside the café here and grab a hot.

Music underscore ends.

GIRL: You got any money?

SLANG TALK MAN: The girl asked and stiffed like a ramrod.

GIRL: Nobody ain't pimping on me. You dig me?

SWEET BACK/JELLY: Aww now baby!

GIRL: I seen you two mullet-heads before. I was uptown when Joe Brown had you all in the go-long last night. That cop sure hates a pimp. All he needs to see is the pimps' salute and he'll out with his night-stick and ship your head to the red. Beat your head just as flat as a dime.

The girl sounds off like a siren. Sweet Back and Jelly rush to silence her.

SWEET BACK: Ah-ah-ah, let's us don't talk about the law. Let's talk about us. About you goin' inside with me to holler, "Let one come flopping! One come grunting! Snatch one from the rear!"

GIRL: Naw indeed. You skillets is trying to promote a meal on me. But it'll never happen, brother. You barking up the wrong tree. I wouldn't give you air if you was stopped up in a jug. I'm not putting out a thing. I'm just like the cemetery. I'm not putting out, I'm takin' in. Dig. I'll tell you like the farmer told the potato—plant you now and dig you later.

Music underscore.

SLANG TALK MAN: The girl made a movement to switch off. Sweet Back had not dirtied a plate since the day before. He made a weak but desperate gesture.

Just as Sweet Back places his hand on her purse, the girl turns to stare him down. Music underscore ends.

GIRL: Trying to snatch my pocketbook, eh?
SLANG TALK MAN: Instead of running . . .

The girl grabs Sweet Back's zoot-suit jacket.

GIRL: How much split you want back here? If your feets don't hurry up and take you 'way from here, you'll ride away. I'll spread my lungs all over New York and call the law.

Jelly moves in to try and calm her.

GIRL: Go ahead. Bedbug! Touch me! I'll holler like a pretty white woman!

The girl lets out three "pretty white woman" screams and then struts off. Music underscores her exit.

SLANG TALK MAN: She turned suddenly and rocked on off, her earring snapping and her heels popping.

SWEET BACK: My people, my people.

SLANG TALK MAN: Jelly made an effort to appear that he had no part in the fiasco.

JELLY: I know you feel chewed.

SWEET BACK: Oh let her go. When I see people without the periodical principles they's supposed to have, I just don't fool with 'em. *(Calling out after her)* What I want to steal her old pocketbook with all the money I got? I could buy a beat chick like you and give you away. I got money's mammy and Grandma's change. One of my women, and not the best one I got neither, is buying me ten shag suits at one time.

He glanced sidewise at Jelly to see if he was convincing.

JELLY: But Jelly's thoughts were far away.

Music underscore.

SLANG TALK MAN: He was remembering those full hot meals he had left back in Alabama to seek wealth and splendor in Harlem without working. He had even forgotten to look cocky and rich.

BLUES SPEAK WOMAN:

I GIT TO THE GIT
WITH SOME PAIN AND SOME SPIT
AND SOME SPUNK

The lights slowly fade.

ACT 2

Danitra Vance and Kevin Jackson in "The Gilded Six-Bits" from the New York Shakespeare Festival production.

SONG: YOU BRINGS OUT THE BOOGIE IN ME

Lights reveal Blues Speak Woman and Guitar Man.

BLUES SPEAK WOMAN:

    I DON'T KNOW WHAT YOU GOT
    BUT IT DON'T TAKE A GENIUS TO SEE
    BUT WHATEVER YOU GOT
    IT'S HOT AND IT'S MELTING ME

GUITAR MAN: Don't hurt yo'self now.

BLUES SPEAK WOMAN:

    WHEN YOU UMMMM LIKE THAT
    AND YOU AHHHH LIKE THAT
    YOU CAN MAKE ME CLIMB DOWN FROM MY
        TREE
    YOUR LOVE HAS SHOOK ME UP
    AND IT BRINGS OUT THE BOOGIE IN ME

GUITAR MAN:

    ALL THE WOMEN I HAD
    THEY WERE GLAD WHEN MY BOOGIE GOT
        TIRED

BLUES SPEAK WOMAN: Ohhh your boogie is callin' me
home.

49

GUITAR MAN:

> THEY WOULD SPUTTER AND SCRATCH
> LIKE A MATCH THAT YOU CAN'T SET ON FIRE
> WHEN YOU OOOOHH LIKE THAT
> AND YOU OHHHH LIKE THAT
> YOU CAN MAKE A BLIND MAN SEE
> YOU'RE A CHOCOLATE COOKIE
> AND YOU BRING OUT THE BOOGIE IN ME

They scat.

GUITAR MAN:

> LET'S GO DOWN TO THE BEACH
> YOU COULD TEACH ME A THING OR TWO

BLUES SPEAK WOMAN:

> WE COULD SPEND ALL OUR TIME
> DRINKIN' WINE IN MY RED TIP CANOE

BLUES SPEAK WOMAN/GUITAR MAN:

> WE COULD UMMMMM . . . LIKE THIS
> WE COULD AHHHHHHH . . . LIKE THIS
> WE COULD SHAKE THE FRUIT DOWN FROM
>   THE TREE
> YOUR LOVE HAS SHOOK ME UP
> AND IT BRINGS OUT THE BOOGIE IN ME

BLUES SPEAK WOMAN:

> YOUR LOVE HAS SHOOK ME UP
> AND IT BRINGS OUT THE BOOGIE IN ME

GUITAR MAN:

> YOUR LOVE HAS SHOOK ME UP
> AND IT BRINGS OUT THE BOOGIE IN ME

BLUES SPEAK WOMAN/GUITAR MAN:

> YOUR LOVE HAS SHOOK ME UP
> AND IT BRINGS OUT THE BOOGIE IN ME!

GUITAR MAN:

> YOUR LOVE
> YOUR LOVE

BLUES SPEAK WOMAN *(Simultaneously)*:

> YOU KNOW IT SHOOK ME
> IT REALLY SHOOK ME UP

GUITAR MAN:

> BRINGS OUT THE BOOGIE

BLUES SPEAK WOMAN:

> BRINGS OUT THE BOOGIE

BLUES SPEAK WOMAN/GUITAR MAN:

> BRINGS OUT THE BOOGIE
> IN ME!

Blackout.

"The Gilded Six-Bits"

Music underscore. Lights reveal the Players, a trio of vaudevillians. They present themselves to the audience. The Man speaks with a grandioso eloquence. The Woman (played by Blues Speak Woman) is voluptuous and refined. The Boy, their assistant, is awkward yet willing. On the Man's cue, the tale begins.

MAN: It was a Negro yard, around a Negro house, in a Negro settlement that looked to the payroll of the G and G Fertilizer works for its support. But there was something happy about the place.

WOMAN: The front yard was parted in the middle by a sidewalk from gate to doorstep.

MAN: A mess of homey flowers . . .

The Woman flashes her floral fan, which becomes the planted flowers.

MAN: . . . planted without a plan bloomed cheerily from their helter-skelter places.

WOMAN: The fence and house were whitewashed. The porch
and steps scrubbed white.

BOY: It was Saturday.

WOMAN: Everything clean from the front gate to the privy
house.

MAN: Yard raked so that the strokes of the rake would make
a pattern.

BOY: Fresh newspaper cut in fancy-edge on the kitchen
shelves.

MAN: The front door stood open to the sunshine so that the
floor of the front room could finish drying after its
weekly scouring.

WOMAN: Missie May . . .

*The Boy lowers a "theatrical curtain" to reveal Missie May, as
if she were bathing.*

WOMAN: Was bathing herself in the galvanized washtub in
the bedroom. Her dark-brown skin . . .

MISSIE: Glistened . . .

WOMAN: Under the soapsuds that skittered down from her
wash rag. Her stiff young breasts . . .

MISSIE: Thrust forward aggressively . . .

WOMAN: Like broad-based cones with tips lacquered in
black.

MISSIE: She heard men's voices in the distance and glanced at
the dollar clock on the dresser.

Humph! Ah'm way behind time t'day! Joe gointer be
heah 'fore Ah git my clothes on if Ah don't make haste.

She grabbed the clean meal sack at hand and dried
herself hurriedly and began to dress.

The Man heralds the entrance of Joe.

MISSIE: But before she could tie her slippers, there came the ring of singing metal on wood . . .

As Joe hurls the coins, the Woman produces the sound of the falling coins by shaking a tambourine.

MISSIE: Nine times!

JOE: Missie grinned with delight. She had not seen the big tall man come stealing in the gate and creep up the walk grinning happily at the joyful mischief he was about to commit.

MISSIE: But she knew it was her husband throwing silver dollars in the door for her to pick up and pile beside her plate at dinner. It was this way every Saturday afternoon.

JOE: The nine dollars hurled into the open door, he scurried to a hiding place behind the cape jasmine bush and waited.

The Boy lifts a branch, bursting with flowers, thereby becoming a tree, which Joe hides behind.

MISSIE: Missie promptly appeared at the door in mock alarm. *(Calling out)* Who dat chunkin' money in mah do'way?

She leaped off the porch and began to search the shrubbery.

JOE: While she did this, the man behind the jasmine darted to the chinaberry tree.

MISSIE: She peeped under the porch and hung over the gate to look up and down the road. She spied him and gave chase. *(Calling out)* Ain't nobody gointer be chunkin' money at me and Ah not do'em nothin'.

As the chase between Missie and Joe ensues . . .

MAN: He ran around the house, Missie May at his heels.

WOMAN: She overtook him at the kitchen door.

BOY: He ran inside but could not close it after him before she . . .

WOMAN: Crowded in and locked with him in a rough and tumble.

MAN: For several minutes the two were a furious mass of male and female energy.

WOMAN: Shouting!

MAN: Laughing!

BOY: Twisting!

WOMAN: Turning!

BOY: Joe trying but not too hard to get away.

JOE: Missie May, take yo' hand outta mah pocket.

MISSIE: Ah ain't, Joe, not lessen you gwine gimme whateve' it is good you got in yo' pocket. Turn it go Joe, do Ah'll tear yo' clothes.

JOE: Go on tear 'em. You de one dat pushes de needles round heah. Move yo' hand Missie May.

MISSIE: Lemme git that paper sack out yo' pocket. Ah bet it's candy kisses.

JOE: Tain't. Move yo' hand. Woman ain't got no business in a man's clothes nohow. Go 'way.

MISSIE: Missie May gouged way down and gave an upward jerk and triumphed.

Unhhunh! Ah got it. And it 'tis so candy kisses. Ah

knowed you had somethin' for me in yo' clothes. Now
Ah got to see whut's in every pocket you got.

JOE: Joe smiled . . . and let his wife go through all of his
pockets and take out the things that he had hidden there
for her to find.

WOMAN: She bore off the chewing gum. The cake of sweet
soap. The pocket handkerchief . . .

BOY: As if she had wrested them from him . . .

AN: As if they had not been bought for the sake of this
friendly battle.

GUITAR MAN/PLAYERS:

YOUR LOVE HAS SHOOK ME UP
AND IT BRINGS OUT THE BOOGIE IN ME
YOUR LOVE HAS SHOOK ME UP
AND IT BRINGS OUT THE BOOGIE IN ME
YOUR LOVE HAS SHOOK ME UP
AND IT BRINGS OUT THE BOOGIE IN ME

*Music underscore ends. The Players are gone and Missie and Joe
are alone. The energy between them changes; from frolicsome to
seductive.*

JOE: Whew! That play-fight done got me all warmed up.
Got me some water in de kittle?

MISSIE: Yo' water is on de fire and yo' clean things is cross de
bed. Hurry up and wash yo'self and git changed so we
kin eat. Ah'm hongry.

JOE: You ain't hongry sugar. Youse jes's little empty. Ah'm
de one with all the hongry. Ah could eat up camp
meetin', back off 'ssociation and drink Jurdan dry. You
have it on de table when Ah git out de tub.

MISSIE: Don't you mess wid my business, man. Ah'm a real

wife, not no dress and breath. Ah might not look lak one, but if you burn me down, you won't git a thing but wife ashes.

Joe splashed in the bedroom and Missie May fanned around in the kitchen. A fresh red and white checked cloth on the table. Big pitcher of buttermilk beaded with pale drops of butter from the churn. Hot fried mullet.

JOE *(Elated)*: Huh?

MISSIE: Crackling bread.

JOE: Ummm?

MISSIE: Ham hocks atop a mound of string beans and new potatoes.

JOE: Ummmm.

MISSIE: And perched on the window-sill . . .

JOE/MISSIE: A pone of spicy potato pudding.

Lights reveal the Players.

MAN: Very little talk during the meal . . .

The Boy presents a tray containing a plate of food, which he places before Missie and Joe.

BOY: Except banter that pretended to deny affection . . .

WOMAN: But in reality flaunted it.

The Boy flips the tray to reveal a plate containing dessert.

JOE *(As if he's just eaten a full meal)*: Ummmm. We goin' down de road a li'l piece t'night so go put on yo' Sunday-go-to-meetin' things.

MISSIE: Sho' nuff, Joe?

JOE: Yeah. A new man done come heah from Chicago. Got a place and took and opened it up for an ice cream parlor, and bein' as it's real swell, Ah wants you to be one of de first ladies to walk in dere and have some set down.

MISSIE: Do Jesus, Ah ain't knowed nothin' 'bout it. Who de man done it?

JOE: Mister Otis D. Slemmons, of spots and places.

Lights reveal the Man, playing the role of Slemmons. Hanging from his vest, gold coins on a chain. Music underscore.

SLEMMONS: Memphis, Chicago, Jacksonville, Philadelphia and so on.

MISSIE: You mean that heavy-set man wid his mouth full of gold teethes?

JOE: Yeah. Where did you see 'im at?

MISSIE: Ah went down to de sto' tuh git a box of lye and Ah seen 'im.

SLEMMONS: Standin' on de corner talkin' to some of de mens.

MISSIE: And Ah come on back and went to scrubbin' de floor, and whilst I was scouring the steps . . .

SLEMMONS: He passed and tipped his hat.

MISSIE: And Ah thought, hmmm, never Ah seen him before.

JOE: Yeah, he's up to date.

SLEMMONS: He got de finest clothes Ah ever seen on a colored man's back.

MISSIE: Aw, he don't look no better in his clothes than you do in yourn. He got a puzzlegut on 'im. And he's so chuckle-headed, he got a pone behind his neck.

JOE: He ain't puzzle-gutted honey. He jes' got a corperation. That make 'm look lak a rich white man. Wisht Ah had a build on me lak he got.

SLEMMONS: All rich mens got some belly on 'em.

MISSIE: Ah seen de pitchers of Henry Ford and he's a spare-built man. And Rockefeller look lak he ain't got but one gut. But Ford, Rockefeller and dis Slemmons and all de rest kin be as many-gutted as dey please. Ah'm satisfied wid you jes' like you is, baby. God took pattern after a pine tree and built you noble. Youse a pritty still man. And if Ah knowed any way to make you mo' pritty still, Ah'd take and do it.

They kiss.

JOE: You jes' say dat cause you love me. But Ah know Ah can't hold no light to Otis D. Slemmons. Ah ain't never been nowhere and Ah ain't got nothin' but you.

MISSIE: How you know dat, Joe?

JOE: He tole us so hisself.

Slemmons moves in and around the scene, his presence never acknowledged by Missie or Joe.

MISSIE: Dat don't make it so. His mouf is cut cross-ways ain't it? Well, he kin lie jes' like anybody else.

JOE: Good Lawd, Missie! He's got a five-dollar gold piece for a stick-pin.

SLEMMONS: And a ten-dollar gold piece for his watch chain.

JOE: And his mouf is jes' crammed full of gold teeth. And whut make it so cool, he got money 'cumulated.

SLEMMONS: And womens give it all to 'im.

MISSIE: Ah don't see whut de womens sees on 'im. Ah wouldn't give 'im a wind if de sherff wuz after 'im.

JOE: Well, he tole us how de white womens in Chicago give 'im all dat gold money.

SLEMMONS: So he don't 'low nobody to touch it. Not even put dey finger on it at all.

JOE: You can make 'miration at it, but don't tetch it.

MISSIE: Whyn't he stay up dere where dey so crazy 'bout 'im?

JOE: Ah reckon dey done make 'im vast-rich and he wants to travel some. He say dey wouldn't leave 'im hit a lick of work.

SLEMMONS: He got mo' lady people crazy 'bout him than he kin shake a stick at.

MISSIE: Joe, Ah hates to see you so dumb. Dat stray nigger jes' tell y'all anything and y'all b'lieve it.

JOE: Go 'head on now, honey and put on yo' clothes. He talkin' 'bout his pritty womens—Ah wants 'im to see mine.

MISSIE: Missie May went off to dress.

As Missie exits, the music fades.

JOE *(Confidentially to the audience)*: And Joe spent the time trying to make his stomach punch out like Slemmons' middle.

MAN: But found that his tall bone-and-muscle stride fitted ill with it.

Music underscore. The Man "becomes" Slemmons and the playing arena, a juke joint. Guitar Man and the Woman are on hand as the entertainment.

SLEMMONS: Hey yaw! Welcome to Otis D. Slemmons Ice Creme Parlor and Fun House!

As Guitar Man/Woman sing, Joe and Missie enter the Parlor.

*He introduces Missie to Slemmons and then grabs her and
begins to dance.*

SONG: TELL ME MAMA

GUITAR MAN/WOMAN:

TELL ME MAMA,

WHAT IS WRONG WITH YOU

   (TELL ME MAMA, WON'TCHA TELL ME

     MAMA)

TELL ME MAMA,

WHAT IS WRONG WITH YOU

   (TELL ME MAMA, WON'TCHA TELL

     ME MAMA)

YOU MUST WANT SOMEBODY

TO LAY DOWN AND DIE FOR YOU

IT RAINED FORTY DAYS

FORTY NIGHTS WITHOUT STOPPIN'

   (JONAH)

JONAH GOT MAD CAUSE

THE RAIN KEPT ON DROPPIN'

   (JONAH)

JONAH RUN AND GOT

IN THE BELLY OF THE WHALE

   (JONAH)

NINETY TIMES I'M GON'

TELL THAT SAME BIG TALE

THE WHALE BEGAN TO WIGGLE

   (JONAH)

JONAH BEGAN TO SCRATCH

   (JONAH)

THE WHALE GO JUMP
IN SOMEONE'S SWEET POTATO PATCH

OH TELL ME MAMA,
WHAT IS WRONG WITH YOU
    (TELL ME MAMA, WON'TCHA TELL
      ME MAMA)
TELL ME MAMA
WHAT IS WRONG WITH YOU
    (TELL ME MAMA, WON'TCHA TELL
      ME MAMA)
YOU MUST WANT SOMEBODY
TO LAY DOWN AND DIE FOR YOU

*Joe, caught up in the music, doesn't notice Slemmons has
grabbed his wife and is now dancing with her. Missie is clearly
mesmerized by Slemmons' "gold."*

GUITAR MAN/WOMAN:
    TWO CHEAP EASY MORGAN,
    RUNNIN' SIDE BY SIDE

Everybody adds in.

ALL:
    TWO CHEAP EASY MORGAN
    RUNNIN' SIDE BY SIDE
    IF YOU CATCH YO'SELF A CHEAPY
    THEY MIGHT AS WELL LET YOU RIDE
    IF YOU CATCH YO'SELF A CHEAPY
    THEY MIGHT AS WELL LET YOU RIDE

    IF YOU CATCH YO'SELF A CHEAPY

THEY MIGHT AS WELL LET YOU . . .
RIDE!

*The number ends. The Players watch the scene between Joe and
Missie.*

JOE: Didn't Ah say ole Otis was swell? Can't he talk Chicago
talk? And know what he tole me when Ah was payin' for
our ice cream? He say—

The Man becomes Slemmons.

SLEMMONS: Ah have to hand it to you, Joe. Dat wife of
yours is jes' thirty-eight and two. Yessuh, she's forty
shakes!

JOE: Ain't he killin'?

MISSIE: He'll do in case of a rush. But he sho' is got uh heap
uh gold on 'im. Dat's de first time Ah ever seed gold
money. It lookted good on him sho' nuff, but it'd look a
whole heap better on you.

JOE: Who me? Missie May was youse crazy! Where would a
po' man lak me git gold money from?

WOMAN: Missie May was silent for a minute.

BOY *(Overlapping)*: Missie May was silent for a minute.

MAN *(Overlapping)*: Missie May was silent for a minute.

MISSIE: Us might find some goin' long de road some time.

Joe laughs.

MISSIE: Us could!

JOE *(Laughing)*: Who would be losin' gold money 'round
heah? We ain't ever seen none of dese white folks wearin'
no gold money on dey watch chain.

MISSIE: You don't know whut been lost 'round heah. Maybe

somebody way back in memorial times lost they gold
money and went on off and it ain't never been found.
And then if we wuz to find it, you could wear some
'thout havin' no gang of womens lak dat Slemmons say
he got.

JOE: Don't be so wishful 'bout me. Ah'm satisfied de way Ah
is. So long as Ah be yo' husband, Ah don't keer 'bout
nothin' else. Ah'd ruther all the other womens in de
world to be dead then for you to have de toothache. *(He
kisses her)* Less we go to bed and git our night's rest.

*Music underscore. As Man and Woman speak, the Boy holds a
fall branch, under which Missie and Joe dance—their moves
sensuous.*

MAN: It was Saturday night once more before Joe could
parade his wife in Slemmons' ice cream parlor.

BOY: He worked the night shift and Saturday was his only
night off.

WOMAN: Every other evening around six o'clock he left home
and dying dawn saw him hustling home around the lake.

MAN: That was the best part of life . . .

WOMAN: Going home to Missie May.

MAN: Their whitewashed house . . .

WOMAN: Their mock battle on Saturday . . .

MAN: Dinner and ice cream parlor afterwards . . .

WOMAN: Church on Sunday nights when Missie outdressed
any woman in town.

Joe kisses Missie goodbye.

JOE *(To the audience)*: Everything was right!

64

MAN: One night around eleven the acid ran out at the G and G.

BOY: The foreman knocked off the crew and let the steam die down.

Lights isolate Joe. During the following sequence the Man and Boy become the voices in Joe's head, his feelings; at times even becoming Joe, mirroring his moves. Even though Missie is discussed, she is not seen during this sequence.

JOE: As Joe rounded the lake on his way home . . .

WOMAN:

A LEAN MOON RODE THE LAKE ON A SILVER BOAT.

MAN: If anybody had asked Joe about the moon on the lake, he would have said he hadn't paid it any attention.

JOE: But he saw it with his feelings. It made him yearn painfully for Missie May.

BOY: Missie May.

JOE: They had been married for more than a year now. They had money put away. They ought to be making little feet for shoes. A little boy child would be about right.

MAN: Be about right.

BOY: He saw a dim light in the bedroom . . .

MAN: And decided to come in through the kitchen door.

JOE: He could wash the fertilizer dust off himself before presenting himself to Missie May. It would be nice for her not to know that he was there until he slipped into his place in bed and hugged her back.

JOE/BOY/MAN: She always liked that!

BOY: He eased the kitchen door open . . .

JOE: Slowly and silently . . .

MAN: But when he went to set his dinner bucket on the table —

JOE: He bumped.

BOY: Into a pile of dishes.

MAN: And something crashed to the floor.

JOE: He heard his wife gasp in fright and hurried to reassure her. *(A hushed voice)* Iss me, honey. Don't get skeered.

MAN: There was a quick large movement in the bedroom.

BOY: A rustle.

MAN: A thud.

BOY: A stealthy silence.

MAN: The lights went out.

JOE *(After a beat)*: What?

BOY: Robbers?

MAN: Murderers?

BOY: Someone attacking your helpless wife, perhaps?

JOE: He struck a match, threw himself on guard and stepped over the door-sill into the bedroom.

WOMAN: The great belt on the wheel of Time slipped. And eternity stood still.

MAN: By the match light he could see . . .

JOE: The man's legs fighting with his breeches in his frantic desire to get them on.

BOY: He had both chance and time to kill the intruder.

JOE: But he was too weak to take action. He was assaulted in his weakness.

MAN: Like Samson awakening after his haircut.

BOY: So he just opened his mouth . . .

JOE: And laughed.

MAN: The match went out.

BOY: He struck another.

MAN: And lit the lamp.

JOE: A howling wind raced across his heart.

MAN AND BOY *(Echoing)*: His heart . . . his heart.

JOE: But underneath its fury he heard his wife sobbing.

MAN: And Slemmons pleading for his life. Offering to buy it
with all that he had. *(As Slemmons)* Please suh, don't kill
me. Sixty-two dollars at de sto' gold money.

JOE: Joe just stood there.

MAN: Slemmons considered a surprise attack.

BOY: But before his fist could travel an inch . . .

JOE: Joe's own rushed out to crush him like a battering ram.
Git into yo' damn rags Slemmons and dat quick!

MAN: Slemmons scrambled to his feet.

JOE: He grabbed at him with his left hand and struck at him
with his right.

MAN: Slemmons was knocked into the kitchen and fled
through the front door.

Music underscore ends.

WOMAN: Joe found himself alone with Missie May, the
golden watch charm clutched in his left hand. A short
bit of broken chain dangled between his fingers.

In isolated light, Missie and Joe, as the Players look on.

MISSIE: Missie May was sobbing.

JOE *(Simultaneously)*: Joe stood and stood.

MISSIE: Wails of weeping without words . . .

JOE *(Simultaneously)*: And felt without thinking . . . and
without seeing with his natural eyes Joe kept on . . .

MISSIE: She kept on crying . . .

JOE *(Simultaneously)*: . . . feeling so much and not knowing what to do with all his feelings.

    Missie May whut you cryin' for?

MISSIE: Cause Ah love you so hard and Ah know you don't love me no mo'.

JOE: You don't know de feelings of dat yet, Missie May.

MISSIE: Oh Joe, honey, he said he was gointer gimme dat gold money and he jes' kept on after me.

JOE: Well don't cry no mo' Miss May. Ah got yo' gold piece for you.

    He put Slemmons' watch charm in his pants pocket and went to bed.

Music underscore.

MAN: The hours went past. Joe still and quiet on one bed rail.

BOY: And Miss May wrung dry of sobs on the other.

WOMAN:

    FINALLY THE SUN'S TIDE
    CREPT UPON THE SHORE OF NIGHT
    AND DROWNED ALL ITS HOURS

MISSIE: Missie May with her face stiff and streaked towards the window saw the dawn come into her yard. It was day, nothing more. Joe wouldn't be coming home as usual. No need to fling open the front door and sweep off the porch, making it nice for Joe. No more breakfast to cook; no more washing and starching of Joe's jumper-jackets and pants. No more nothing.

JOE: No more nothing.

MISSIE: So why get up. With this strange man in her bed, Missie felt embarrassed to get up and dress. She decided to wait till he had dressed and gone. Then she would get

up, dress quickly and be gone forever beyond reach of
Joe's looks and laughs. But he never moved.

JOE: He never moved.

MISSIE: Red light turned to yellow, then white.

WOMAN: From beyond the no-man's land between them came
a voice.

Music underscore ends.

MAN: A strange voice that yesterday had been Joe's.

JOE: Missie May ain't you gonna fix me no breakfus'?

MISSIE: She sprang out of bed.

  Yeah Joe. Ah didn't reckon you wuz hongry.

  No need to die today. Joe needed her for a few more
minutes anyhow.

WOMAN: Soon there was a roaring fire in the cook stove.

MAN: Water bucket full and two chickens killed.

BOY: She rushed hot biscuits to the table as Joe took his seat.

JOE: He ate with his eyes on his plate.

WOMAN: No laughter, no banter.

JOE: Missie May you ain't eatin' yo' breakfus'?

MISSIE: Ah don't choose none, Ah thank yuh.

JOE: His coffee cup was empty.

MISSIE: She sprang to refill it.

BOY: When she turned from the stove and bent to set the
cup beside Joe's plate, she saw . . .

MISSIE: The yellow coin on the table between them.

GUITAR MAN/PLAYERS:

  THE SUN CAME UP
  AND THE SUN WENT DOWN
  THE SUN CAME UP
  AND THE SUN WENT DOWN

Guitar Man maintains the above chant as isolated pools of light reveal Missie and Joe. The Players chronicle the passage of time with their movements.

WOMAN: The sun, the hero of every day, the impersonal old man that beams as brightly on death as on birth, came up every morning and raced across the blue dome and dipped into the sea of fire every evening.

MAN: Water ran down hill.

BOY: Birds nested.

WOMAN: But there were no more Saturday romps.

MAN: No ringing silver dollars to stack beside her plate.

MISSIE: No pockets to rifle.

WOMAN: In fact the yellow coin in his trousers was like a monster hiding in the cave of his pockets to destroy her.

MAN: She often wondered if he still had it but nothing could have induced her to ask nor explore his pockets to see for herself.

BOY: Its shadow was in the house whether or no.

GUITAR MAN/PLAYERS:
THE SUN CAME UP
AND THE SUN WENT DOWN
THE SUN CAME UP
AND THE SUN WENT DOWN

MISSIE: She knew why she didn't leave Joe. She couldn't. She loved him too much. But she couldn't understand why Joe didn't leave her. He was polite, even kind at times, but aloof.

GUITAR MAN/PLAYERS:
THE SUN CAME UP
AND THE SUN WENT DOWN

THE SUN CAME UP
AND THE SUN WENT DOWN

MAN: One night Joe came home around midnight . . .

JOE: Complained of pains in the back. He asked Missie to rub him down with liniment.

MISSIE: It had been three months since Missie had touched his body and it all seemed strange. But she rubbed him. Grateful for the chance.

JOE: Before morning, youth triumphed . . .

MISSIE: And Missie exulted.

GUITAR MAN/PLAYERS:

THE SUN CAME UP
AND THE SUN WENT DOWN
THE SUN CAME UP
AND THE SUN WENT DOWN

BOY: But the next day beneath her pillow she found . . .

MISSIE: The piece of money with the bit of chain attached.

WOMAN: She took it into her hands with trembling and saw first that it was no gold piece.

MAN: It was a gilded half-dollar.

MISSIE: Then she knew why Slemmons had forbidden anyone to touch his gold.

WOMAN: He trusted village eyes at a distance not to recognize his stick-pin as a gilded quarter.

BOY: And his watch charm as a four-bit piece.

MISSIE: She was glad at first that Joe had left it there. Perhaps he was through with her punishment. They were man and wife again.

MAN: Then another thought came clawing at her.

MISSIE: He had come home to buy from her as if she were any woman in the long house. As if to say that he could

71

pay as well as Slemmons. She slid the coin into his Sunday pants pocket and dressed herself and left his house. Halfway between her house and the quarters, she met her husband's mother . . .

Missie finds herself trapped in the severe gaze of the Woman who has "become" Joe's mother.

MISSIE: And after a short talk she turned and went back home. If she had not the substance of marriage, she had the outside show. Joe must leave *her*. She let him see she didn't want his old gold four-bits too.

GUITAR MAN/PLAYERS:

> THE SUN CAME UP
> AND THE SUN WENT DOWN
> THE SUN CAME UP
> AND THE SUN WENT DOWN

MISSIE: She saw no more of the coin for some time though she knew that Joe could not help finding it in his pocket. But his health kept poor . . .

JOE: And he came home at least every ten days . . .

MISSIE: To be rubbed.

GUITAR MAN:

> THE SUN WENT DOWN
> THE SUN CAME UP
> THE SUN WENT DOWN

WOMAN:

> THE SUN SWEPT AROUND THE HORIZON
> TRAILING ITS ROBES OF WEEKS AND DAYS

GUITAR MAN:

> THE SUN CAME UP.

The Woman tosses snow into the air as the Boy lifts a barren branch. It is now winter. Music underscore ends as Joe stands before a very pregnant Missie.

JOE: One morning Joe came in from work, he found Missie May chopping wood. Without a word he took the ax and chopped a huge pile before he stopped. *(To Missie)* You ain't got no business choppin' wood and you know it.

MISSIE: How come? Ah been choppin' it for de last longest.

JOE: Ah ain't blind. You makin' feet for shoes.

MISSIE: Won't you be glad to have a li'l baby child Joe?

JOE: You know dat 'thout astin' me.

MISSIE: Iss gointer be a boy chile and de very spit of you.

JOE: You reckon Missie May?

MISSIE: Who else could it look lak?

JOE: Joe said nothing.

MISSIE: But thrust his hand deep into his pocket and fingered something.

Music underscore.

MAN: It was almost three months later Missie May took to bed.

BOY: And Joe went and got his mother to come wait on the house.

Lights reveal Missie and the Woman, as Joe's mother, assisting Missie as she gives birth. The Woman hums/moans Missie's pain, which builds to a gospel wail, until . . .

WOMAN: Missie May delivered a fine boy.

Music underscore ends.

BOY: When Joe came in from work one morning—

MAN: His mother and the old women were drinking great bowls of coffee around the fire in the kitchen.

Joe crosses to his mother. The Man looks on.

JOE: How did Missie May make out?

MOTHER: Who, dat gal? She strong as a ox. She gointer have plenty mo'. We done fixed her wid de sugar and lard to sweeten her for de nex' one.

MAN: Joe stood silent.

MOTHER: You ain't ast 'bout de baby Joe. You oughter be mighty proud cause he sho' is de spittin' image of yuh, son. Dat's yourn all right, if you never git another one, dat un is yourn.

Joe grabs his mother, hugs her, lets out a shout.

MOTHER: And you know Ah'm mighty proud too, son, cause Ah never thought well of you marryin' Missie May cause her ma used tuh fan her foot 'round right smart and Ah been mighty skeered dat Missie May wuz gointer git misput on her road. Bless you son.

She exits.

JOE: Joe said nothing.

Music underscore.

JOE: He fooled around the house till late in the day then just before he went to work, he went and stood at the foot of the bed and asked his wife how she felt.

MISSIE: He did this every day during the week.

74

WOMAN: On Saturday he went to Orlando to make his market.

MAN: Way after while he went around to the candy store.

The Boy appears as the clerk, his voice, manner and the mask he wears suggestive of a "Southern Cracker."

CLERK: Hello Joe, the clerk greeted him. Ain't seen you in a long time.

JOE: Nope. Ah ain't been heah. Been 'round spots and places.

CLERK: Want some of them molasses kisses you always buy?

JOE: Yessuh. Will this spend?

CLERK: Whut is it Joe? Well I'll be doggone! A gold-plated four-bit piece. Where'd you git it Joe?

JOE: Offen a stray nigger dat come through Eatonville. He had it on his watch chain for a charm—goin' 'round making out iss gold money. Ha ha! He had a quarter on his tie pin and it wuz all golded up too. Tryin' to fool people. Makin' out he so rich and everything. Tryin' to tole off folkses wives from home.

CLERK: How did you git it Joe? Did he fool you too?

JOE: Who me? Naw suh! He ain't fooled me none. Know whut Ah done? He come 'round wid his smart talk and Ah hauled off and knocked 'im down and took his old four-bits 'way from 'im. Gointer buy my wife some good ole 'lasses kisses wid it. Gimme fifty cents worth of dem candy kisses.

CLERK: Fifty cents buy a mightly lot of candy kisses, Joe. Why don't you split it up and take some chocolate bars, too. They eat good, too.

JOE: Yessuh, dey do, but Ah wants all dat in kisses. Ah got

75

a li'l boy chile home now. Tain't a week old yet, but he kin suck a sugar tit and maybe eat one them kisses hisself.

CLERK: Joe got his candy and left the store. The clerk turned to the next customer.

Wisht I could be like these darkies. Laughin' all the time. Nothin' worries 'em.

The Man, Woman and Boy each make grand entrances, signaling the story is about to end.

MAN: Back in Eatonville . . .

WOMAN: Joe reached his own front door.

BOY: There was a ring of singing metal on wood.

As Joe tosses the coins, the Woman shakes the tambourine.

JOE: Fifteen times!

MISSIE: Missie May couldn't run to the door, but she crept there as quickly as she could.

Joe Banks, Ah hear you chunkin' money in mah do'way. You wait till Ah got mah strength back and Ah'm gointer fix you for dat.

GUITAR MAN:

THE SUN CAME UP

PLAYERS:

I GIT TO THE GIT

GUITAR MAN:

THE SUN WENT DOWN

PLAYERS:

WITH SOME PAIN N' SOME SPIT
N' SOME . . .

GUITAR MAN:

THE SUN CAME UP.

PLAYERS:

SPUNK.

*On the word "spunk," Missie and Joe kiss, their figures cast in
silhouette. The Man gestures. The tale has ended. Blackout.*

END OF PLAY

GLOSSARY FOR "STORY IN HARLEM SLANG"

AIR OUT: leave, flee, stroll.

ASTORPERIOUS: haughty, biggity.

'BAM, DOWN IN 'BAM: down South.

BEATING UP YOUR GUMS: talking to no purpose.

BULL-SKATING: bragging.

COLLAR A NOD: sleep.

COAL-SCUTTLE BLOND: black woman.

CUT: doing something well.

DIDDY-WAH-DIDDY: (1) a far place, a measure of distance; (2) another suburb of Hell, built since way before Hell wasn't no bigger than Baltimore. The folks in Hell go there for a big time.

DUMB TO THE FACT: "You don't know what you're talking about."

FRAIL EEL: pretty girl.

GINNY GALL: a suburb of Hell, a long way off.

GRANNY GRUNT: a mythical character to whom most questions may be referred.

I DON'T DEAL IN COAL: "I don't keep company with black women."

JIG: Negro, a corrupted shortening of Zigaboo.

JELLY: sex.

JULY JAM: something very hot.

JUMP SALTY: get angry.

KITCHEN MECHANIC: a domestic.

MANNY: a term of insult; never used in any other way by Negroes.

MISS ANNE: a white woman.

MY PEOPLE! MY PEOPLE!: sad and satiric expression in the Negro language; sad when a negro comments on the backwardness of some members of his race; at other times, used for satiric or comic effect.

PE-OLA: a very white Negro girl.

PIANO: spareribs (white rib bones suggest piano keys).

PLAYING THE DOZENS: low-rating the ancestors of your opponent.

REEFER: a marijuana cigarette, also a drag.

RIGHTEOUS MOSS OR GRASS: good hair.

RUSSIAN: a southern Negro up North. "Rushed up here," hence a Russian.

SCRAP-IRON: cheap liquor.

SOLID: perfect.

STANCH or STANCH OUT: to begin, commence, step out.

SUGAR HILL: northwest sector of Harlem, near Washington Heights; site of the newest apartment houses, mostly occupied by professional people. (The expression has been distorted in the South to mean a Negro red-light district.)

THE BEAR: confession of poverty.

THOUSAND ON A PLATE: beans.

WHAT·S ON DE RAIL FOR THE LIZARD?: suggestion for moral turpitude.

ZIGABOO: a Negro.

ZOOT SUIT WITH THE REET PLEAT: Harlem-style suit with padded shoulders, 43-inch trousers at the knee with cuff so small it needs a zipper to get into, high waistline, fancy lapels, bushels of buttons, etc.

MUSIC

Ann Duquesnay and Chic Street Man in the New York Shakespeare Festival production.

Jurden Water

DELIA,
ENSEMBLE AND
ACOUSTIC GUITAR

BY CHIC STREET MAN

I've Been Livin' with the Blues

GUITAR MAN
AND ACOUSTIC GUITAR

ARRANGED BY
CHIC STREET MAN

SHAMED PEO-PLE AIN'T THAT NEWS YOU SEE I BEEN LIV-IN' WITH THE

B   C   C⁶/₉   D⁷

BLUES EVER BEEN DOWN YOU KNOW HOW I

G   G E♭⁷ D⁷   G

FEEL I FEEL LIKE AN EN-GINE AIN'T GOT NO DRIV-IN' WHEEL M'NOT A-

G   C   C

SHAMED PEO-PLE AIN'T THAT NEWS___ YOU SEE I BEEN LIV-IN' WITH THE

B   C   C⁶/₉   D⁷

BLUES LORD THE ROCKS HAVE BEEN MY PIL-LOW AND

G   G⁶ G⁷   C   G

87

COLD GROUND HAS BEEN MY BED WELL, BLUE SKIES ___ HAVE BEEN MY

BLANKET AND THE MOON-LIGHT HAS BEEN MY ___ SPREAD

Guitar solo — improvise

OH THE ROCKS HAVE BEEN MY PIL-LOW AND

COLD GROUND HAS BEEN MY BED WELL, BLUE SKIES ___ HAVE BEEN MY

BLAN-KET AND THE MOON-LIGHT HAS BEEN MY ___ SPREAD I

WORKS ALL SUM-MER I SLEEPS ALL FALL I SPEND MY CHRIST-MAS IN MY OVER

-ALLS I'M NOT A- SHAMED PEO-PLE AIN'T THAT NEWS YOU SEE

I BEEN LIV-IN' WITH THE BLUES MY MOM-MA HAD 'EM MY DAD-DY HAD 'EM

TOO YES HE DID I BEEN LIV-IN' WITH THE BLUES 'N THEN

89

ALL YOU OUT THERE TOO WE'VE ALL BEEN LIV-IN' WITH THE

BLUES

Hey Lady

GUITAR MAN,
BLUES SPEAK WOMAN
AND ACOUSTIC GUITAR

BY CHIC STREET MAN

Moderate

MAN: 1. HEY BA-BY
MAN: 2. HEY BABY

BA-BY HOW DO YOU DO?
WHO DO YOU THINK I AM?

BSW: You talkin' to me?

YEAH
BSW: HEY

BA-BY, SAY
BA-BY, JUST

-LY   SLIGHT- LY ___   AND OOH SO PO-LITE-

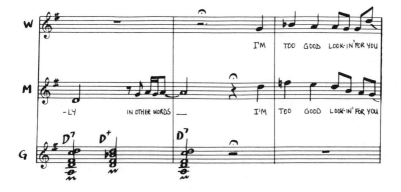

I'M TOO GOOD LOOK-IN' FOR YOU

-LY   IN OTHER WORDS ___   I'M TOO GOOD LOOK-IN' FOR YOU

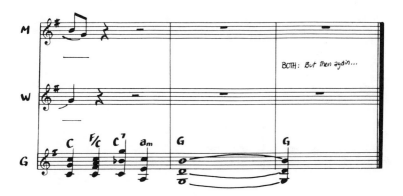

BOTH: But then again...

93

You Brings out the Boogie in Me

BLUES SPEAK WOMAN,
GUITAR MAN AND
ACOUSTIC GUITAR

ARRANGED BY
CHIC STREET MAN

_ TAKE A GE-NIUS TO SEE BUT WHAT-EV-

Alright! I like that!

-ER YOU GOT IT'S HOT AND IT'S MEL-TIN' ME

Don't hurt yourself baby!

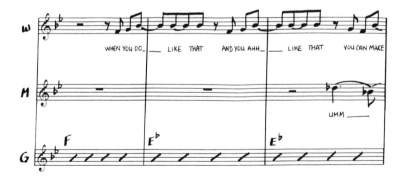

WHEN YOU OO__ LIKE THAT AND YOU AHH__ LIKE THAT YOU CAN MAKE

UMM __

95

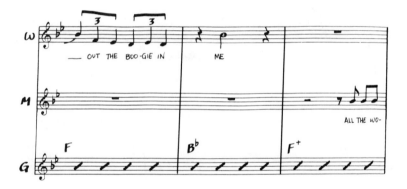

THEY WOULD SPUT- TER AND SCRATCH LIKE A MATCH ___THAT YOU CAN'T SET ON FIRE

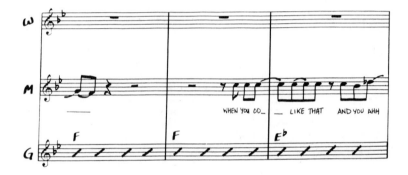

WHEN YOU OO___ ___ LIKE THAT AND YOU AHH

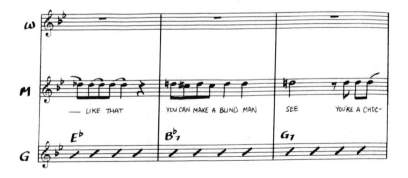

___ LIKE THAT YOU CAN MAKE A BLIND MAN SEE YOU'RE A CHOC-

98

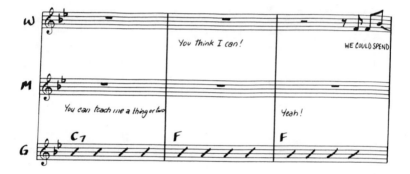

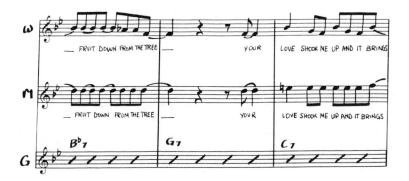

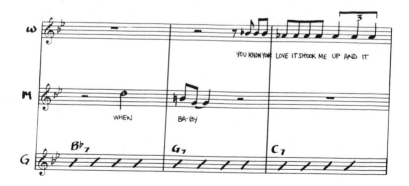

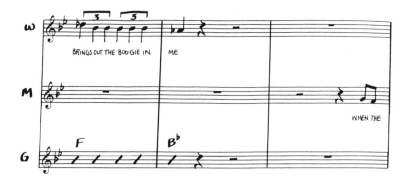

Tell Me Mama!

GUITAR MAN,
HARMONICA AND
ACOUSTIC GUITAR

ARRANGED BY
CHIC STREET MAN

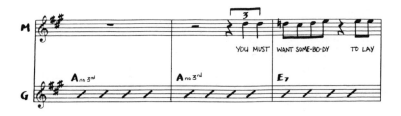

DOWN AND DIE FOR YOU___ 'CAUSE IT RAINED

FOR-TY DAYS AND FORTY NIGHTS WITH-OUT STOP-PIN' JO-NAH GOT MAD 'CAUSE THE RAIN

KEPT ON DROP-PIN' JO- NAH WENT IN THE BEL-LY OF A WHALE

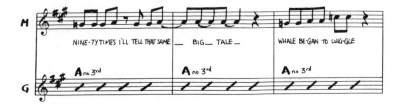

NINE-TY TIMES I'LL TELL THAT SAME ___ BIG___ TALE___ WHALE BE-GAN TO WIG-GLE

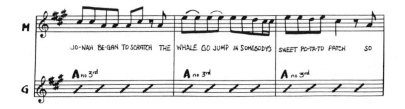

JO-NAH BE-GAN TO SCRATCH THE WHALE GO JUMP IN SOMEBODY'S SWEET PO-TA-TO PATCH SO

105

TELL ME MA-MA WHAT IS WRONG WITH YOU

D7   D7   A no 3rd

SO TELL ME MA-__MA__ WHAT__ IS__ WRONG__ WITH YOU

A no 3rd   D7   D7

YOU MUST WANT SOME-BO-DY TO LAY

A no 3rd   A no 3rd   E7

DOWN AND DIE FOR YOU__ __   LORD TWO__ CHEAP__ EA-

E7   A no 3rd   A no 3rd

-SY__ MOR-__GAN__   RUN-NIN' SIDE BY SIDE__

D7   D7   A

LORD TWO__ CHEAP__ EA·__ __ SY__ MOR·__ GAN__ RUN·NIN' SIDE BY SIDE__

IF YOU CAN'T CATCH __ YOUR·SELF A CHEAP·Y __ THEY

MIGHT AS WELL LET__ YOU RIDE

Harmonica:

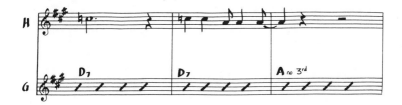

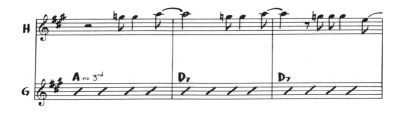

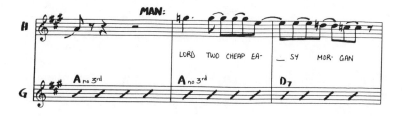

RUN-NIN' SIDE BY SIDE___ LORD TWO CHEAP EA-

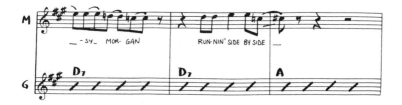

___SY_ MOR-GAN RUN-NIN' SIDE BY SIDE ___

IF YOU CAN'T CATCH YOUR-SELF A CHEAP-Y THEY MIGHT AS WELL LET YOU RIDE

IF YOU CAN'T CATCH YOUR-SELF A CHEAP-Y___ THEY

MIGHT AS WELL LET YOU RIDE ___ ___

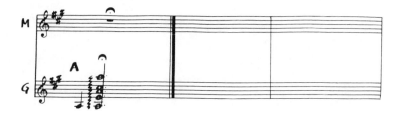

Spunk Tag

GUITAR MAN,
ENSEMBLE AND
ACOUSTIC GUITAR

BY CHIC STREET MAN

YOU KNOW THE SUN CAME UP ALL: (I GIT TO THE GIT) AND THE SUN WENT DOWN WITH SOME PAIN 'N' SOME SPIT AND SOME SPUNK _____

110

ABOUT THE AUTHOR

Zora Neale Hurston (1903–1960), novelist, dramatist and folklorist, was born and raised in Eatonville, Florida, the first incorporated all-black town in America. She attended Howard University in Washington, D.C. and studied anthropology with Franz Boas at both Barnard College and Columbia University in New York City. Anthropological reasearches in her native South provided the basis for all of her writings, which were and remain extremely controversial due to their unflinching—some would say stereotypical—portrayal of African Americans.

Despite early success and a close association with the artists of the Harlem Renaissance, Hurston died poor and forgotten. Rediscovery in the seventies by feminist scholars and writers has led to a fuller appreciation of her standing in American letters and burgeoning production and publication activities.

Her major works include the novel *Their Eyes Were Watching God* and an autobiography, *Dust Tracks on a Road*.

ABOUT THE ADAPTER

George C. Wolfe was born in Frankfort, Ky. in 1954. He is the author of *The Colored Museum,* which premiered at Crossroads Theatre Company in 1986 as that theatre's winner of the CBS/FDG New Play Award, and was subsequently produced by the New York Shakespeare Festival and the Royal Court Theatre, London, as well as by numerous regional theatres across the U.S. He co-directed a television production of the play for PBS-TV's *Great Performances.* Wolfe has written the book and directed the musical *Jelly's Last Jam,* which had its premiere at the Mark Taper Forum, and a teleplay, *Hunger Chic,* for the PBS comedy anthology *Trying Times.* He has received grants from the Rockefeller Foundation, the National Institute for Music Theater and the National Endowment for the Arts, and he is on the Executive Council of the Dramatists Guild. He is an artistic associate at the New York Shakespeare Festival. Awards include the Hull-Warriner, the George Oppenheimer/Newsday and an Audelco as well as an Obie for his direction of *Spunk*.

ABOUT THE COMPOSER

Chic Street Man is a singer, songwriter and musical Ambassador for Peace and Human Rights. He has recorded and toured throughout France and other parts of Europe and directed and toured with two *Peace Child* shows to the Soviet Union. He works with children and adults through his workshop in the performing arts to build self-confidence and self-esteem and recently appeared in concert at the General Assembly of the United Nations.